Table o

Introduction ....
Hoorfrost ....
Stitch and Witch 31
The Blue Hour.. 41
The Harp's Voice 61
Acknowledgements 69
About Narrelle M. Harris 71
Other books by Narrelle M. Harris 73

Tales of the Minstrel Tongue

Narrelle M. Harris

Published by Dangerous Charm in 2024

Dangerous Charm
507/225 Elizabeth Street
Melbourne, VIC, 3000
Australia

All rights reserved. No part of this book may be reproduced or transmitted in any form or by any means, including internet search engines and retailers, electronic or mechanical, photocopying (except under the provisions of the Australian Copyright Act 1968), recording or by any information storage and retrieval system, without prior permission in writing from the publisher.

"Hoorfrost" first appeared in Scar Tissue and Other Stories (2019)

The remaining stories first appeared 2020-2023 at Narrelle M Harris' Patreon at:

https://www.patreon.com/NarrelleMHarris

All stories © 2024 Narrelle M. Harris

Cover designed by Narrelle M. Harris, using Canva.

Tales of the Minstrel Tongue

Narrelle M. Harris

Introduction

THE CONCEPT OF 'THE minstrel tongue' is the central conceit of my novel, Kitty and Cadaver, which is about a rock and roll band that fights monsters using the magic that manifests when they sing. This particular band has its roots in the 13th century, when a drummer and a piper join forces to survive a brutal English winter and deal with its supernatural cause.

Through the "grandfather's axe" principle, members of the music troupes and bands that follow come and go, changing their name with every new leader, but they stretch in a line from Will and Thomas in England in 1258, all the way Kitty Carrasco and her band in Melbourne in the 21st century.

NARRELLE M. HARRIS

But these musicians aren't the only ones with magic powers linked to creativity as part of the universe's plan to balance dark forces with more positive ones. The Minstrel Tongue is most common, followed by Estampie Feet ("estampie" is a medieval form of dance and music). But crafters are also able to imbue their creations with magic – like the yarnworkers in 'Stitch and Witch'. Around the world, in the Minstrelverse, are people who can maintain the balance through song and dance, craft and art, in all its forms. I aim to write more about these magicians too.

In the meantime here are a few tales of those blessed (or cursed) with the Minstrel Tongue and its related gifts. Please enjoy them, and look for the magic in the music in your life.

Narrelle M. Harris
Melbourne, 2024

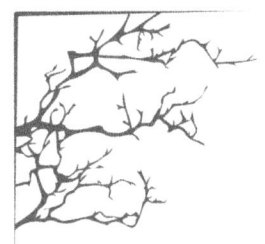

Hoorfrost

L ondon. June. 1258.

'God's *nails!*' Will swore as he trudged through the fresh fall of snow. He suspected he'd wandered off the road to the Ludgate. Surely this grove of elms was further west than he meant to be? He couldn't see the sun, much less any shadows, to judge the time in this milky light, but it must be no later than the third hour, barely half way to noon.

He cursed as his feet crunched down.

God curse this winter and the famine that it brings; God pity the thousands dead for want of food. God curse the frozen Thames and the strange skies of this unspeakable winter. God curse the even stranger thing that lurks in the river's mud.

And triple curse this cocking *snow that will not cease falling.*

When cursing didn't help, Will tried to spell it warmer with a rhythm.

Un-freeze, damn'd-dirt, God's-heart, it's-cold.

His teeth chattered too hard for the chant to be spoken, and numb with cold as he was, it was a poor chant. The result was weak – he never could make much use of water; earth responded best to his call – but the beat of it kept his body moving, less cold than if he stood still. He'd have unslung his tabor, but the skin of it was brittle with frost. Even encased in fur gloves, his hands were stiff. At least he had boots, and the moss stuffed in the left stopped the snow leeching in through the hole and biting his heel.

Having no lodgings, St Martin Le Grand's curfew knell last night had forced Will to sleep beyond the city walls or risk prison. He'd sheltered in St Bartholomew's Priory – its founder had been a minstrel, and the brothers there had given him water and a bite of what little bread they had. This morning he'd left, hoping to find some scraps.

But the bells of St Martin le Grand hadn't rung to herald the opening of the markets, and that was how William Hawk knew he no longer had a choice in what he did next. Whether the problem was no bell, or no markets, the silence meant this unnatural winter was deepening and a cold and hungry death was coming for them all.

If anyone but Will knew what was causing it – that thing in the river – they weren't doing anything. He didn't know what to do either, but he would make his way back into the city to do it. If the church was wrong and God loved him after all, he would succeed.

A sweet, fluting sound pierced Will's cursing and he halted, listening.

TALES OF THE MINSTREL TONGUE

It was the trill of a pipe, played dancingly by a musician of rare skill. Will felt warmer just hearing it. And then his fingers ached less. Will grinned with sudden certainty. He followed the music through the woods and paused when he found its source.

A young man knelt on the ground in a circle of bare earth, playing his pipe. The melody was intricate, dancing swiftly through flurries of notes. The melody line was strong and the notes around it did not rise and fall so much as build and flicker.

In the centre of the ring of earth was a fire, small but bright, fuelled only by air and music. The ground on which the piper sat was dry, but beyond him the snow was pristine, freshly fallen white, marked with the footprints that showed the way by which the piper had come.

Will stepped out of the shelter of the trees.

'God give you good day, friend.'

The music stopped abruptly and the young man rose, his wooden whistle clutched in his left hand, a knife in his right. His stark glare was equal parts anger and fear.

Will held up his hands, palm out.

'Peace, friend. I too am a musician,' he gestured to the drumsticks tucked into his belt. 'Shall I play for you?' He reached slowly for the sticks without waiting for a reply.

The other did not lower his knife, or move, or speak.

Will fetched his sticks but didn't unhitch his tabor. He knelt. With the side of his hand, he pushed aside the snow to reveal the frozen ground. He pulled the gloves off his chapped red hands, took up his sticks, and beat the ground with one stick, then the other.

'Look to your fire, good fellow,' he said, and sang as he played the tattoo.

NARRELLE M. HARRIS

Slumber not, oh root and seed
for Winter has now overstayed
Earth bring forth thy buried tinder
Let fire feed; the frostbite hinder

The fire feeding on air was fading, but the ground beneath it was heaving, cracking, as the fallen branches of the autumn and early winter broke through, pushed on the backs of shifting roots. The fire licked down towards the dry wood and took hungry hold. It crackled and burned brighter.

The heartbeat drum, the breathing fife
We play to ask you give us life
The strength you had when spring did turn
Release as bones of trees to burn

And flamed higher still.

Will stopped playing and the cosy fire feasted on the fuel that the earth had given them.

'We are brothers,' said Will to the astonished man. 'Fear no harm from me.'

The man considered this, then finally put away his knife. 'Sit by the fire, then. Maybe we'll be friends. My name is Thomas Rowan.'

'And I'm William Hawk. The friends I once had called me Will.' He sat next to Thomas Rowan by the fire.

'You once had?'

TALES OF THE MINSTREL TONGUE

'Most are dead now,' Will said. 'Famine and disease, mostly, though sheer cold took its share. My fellows in music. They froze to death on the road a week ago. I dared the charge of heresy and witchcraft to keep us warm and alive, but they fled in terror of me.' Will stared into the fire. 'And therefore are too dead to denounce me a heretic.'

Thomas shifted restlessly. 'My brother had a lovely voice,' he said at last, his own dark with sorrow. 'He tried to sing some safety for us in Lord Hanley's hall, but Hanley hadn't enough to feed us either, so now Dickon is lying with all the others at Spitalfields, waiting for the ground to thaw enough for burials. I hoped to find some other fortune before I joined him as food for worms.'

'I'm sorry for your grief, brother Thomas.'

'And I for yours, brother Will. Where are you going now? Or are you, like me, walking towards death rather than wait for it to come hunting?'

'Walking towards death, I suppose. This winter's taken everything I had, but there's a cause for this bitter season. Something sits in the mud beneath the Thames. I fear it's addled with some ancient, raging sorrow. I feel it when I play the earth. I don't think it means to destroy us, but this strange winter has woken it.'

'You sound sorry for it.' Thomas was not pleased.

'Not really,' said Will. 'The death it brings may not be its intent, but death it brings all the same.'

'You think to kill it?'

'I don't know what it is; still less if it can die. I thought I might try to sing it back to sleep.'

'And if it doesn't want to sleep?'

'I die. But I'll die regardless, in this cold. I'd rather die trying to live.'

Thomas considered this philosophy with a frown.

'How will you make it sleep?'

'I could sing a cradlesong to it. I've sent many to sleep in my time as a minstrel, but that's only ale and my voice.' Will laughed wryly and his breath puffed in cloud. 'I can sing a little magic, but it speaks best through my tabor. Usually I use it to keep bugs from biting, or dry the ground when it rains. Little tricks that hurt none and comfort only me. But I once drummed a stalking wolf into curling like a puppy at my feet, and when I was a boy, a spirit rose from a ruined hall and tried to possess my father. I beat the stones with my hands and sang the ghost to pieces. This thing is doubtless stronger than wolves and ghosts, but I'll die fighting it rather than starve or be frozen blue at the side of the road. What say you?'

'My pipe isn't as clever as Dickon's voice was, but it's yours for this. I've a knife as well.'

'Any tool is useful,' agreed Will.

THE CITY GATES WERE open but untended. Will and Thomas, filled with disquiet, passed through the Ludgate without hindrance. Without fish to sell, the old fish market was silent. Theirs were the only footprints in Thames Street. The only sound was the caw of a raven to the northwest, where Wall Brook was as frozen as the rest.

TALES OF THE MINSTREL TONGUE

The quality of the milky light seemed unchanging, but Will thought he felt the dusk descending by the time they reached the place where the riverbanks crackled with wrongness. The Thames was frozen from shore to shore. Spanning the ice was the London Bridge, built in stone under the reign of King Henry's father, King John. The Chapel of St Thomas on the Bridge stood lonely in the centre. The Brethren of the Bridge who prayed there were either all at prayer or huddled before fires in their Bridge House. Or perhaps they were dead like so many others. Will saw none, wherever they were.

Thomas had shoved his gloved hands into his armpits in an attempt to keep warm.

'Where is it then, this angry, grieving monster?' Thomas's scowl suggested he had an angry, grieving monster of his own, furled underneath his heart.

'Somewhere near. I can feel it when I drum.'

Thomas stamped his feet on the snow. Nothing came to the summons. 'You say the strange winter woke it,' said Thomas. 'Didn't the monster cause this hell?'

Will knelt on the ground with his tabor. 'That's not what the earth tells me.'

For a man who had woven fire out of air with a fife, Thomas was sceptical. 'You talk to the soil often, do you?'

'The earth's a good listener,' replied Will, unruffled. 'She holds many secrets, and sometimes she shares them with me.'

'What's the secret of this killing winter, then?'

Will pushed the snow aside, took off his glove and placed his hand on the bare ground. 'The earth is round, did you know? Full ripe round like an apple but she has a fire at her heart. Sometimes the fire bursts through her skin. She has burning mountains that birth burning rocks, and the smoke of her womb covers the sky.'

'Mountains have burned and spat rocks and smoke before,' said Thomas, 'But winter has only been winter.'

'This particular mountain burst like nothing before it,' said Will solemnly. 'Do you remember the red sunsets in the spring? Colours as violent as blood, the sun lighting on the smoke from the other side of the world? In that fire's wake, summer never came; then winter came and stayed.'

'I was here for those sunsets too,' said Thomas drily. 'For the failed harvests, the dying cattle, the floods that washed away what little had grown, and then froze the rest.'

'Well, that's what woke the thing that slept in the river's mud. It's been here longer than that, of course. Hundreds of years.'

'Does the mud tell you that?'

'It does.' Will rested his hands on his haunches and cocked an eye at Thomas, who glared at the road of ice where a river once ran. 'Curb your anger, Brother Thomas. I didn't make the mountains burn, the skies turn red or the river freeze. I only listen to what the magic tells me.'

Thomas's eyes did not shift from the Thames. 'Shall I tell you what the air says?'

'I'd be most interested to hear.'

'I hear a lament, William. A voice colder than the frozen wastes of the Viking north cries for Baldr, whoever that may be. It begs forgiveness and for punishment for Hoor. For itself.'

TALES OF THE MINSTREL TONGUE

Will listened with all his body and thought he heard something of the lament. A cry crackling with cold; the sound of ice breaking like a heart.

'I hear it. It must have done something terrible, to sound so.'

'I'd offer it punishment, if I could,' said Thomas.

'You have no pity for the thing?'

'It killed my sister.'

'Brother, you said.'

'Both,' growled Thomas.

Grief and rage, thought Will, are not the purview of monsters alone.

'What now?' demanded Thomas.

'I never heard this cry before, and I've often passed this way. The ash sky brought winter early and woke the owner of this voice, to cry out. Its lament is what makes the winter last so long. I'll sing a cradlesong, I think.'

'We should kill it.' Thomas's knife was in his hand again.

'Are you very determined to die?' Will asked gently. 'For I think that taking your little blade to this creature will accomplish that nicely. If you're not so very set on dying, though, I thinking putting it back to sleep may give us a better chance of seeing tomorrow.'

'What should we do, then?'

Will wouldn't admit that he didn't know. All his small magics hadn't prepared him for the task he'd taken on. Instinct told him to connect to the earth, however, so he walked to the edge of the frozen Thames and kneeled on the ice-hard mud. After a moment, Thomas joined him.

Will began with a tattoo drummed on the ground and Thomas began to play a warm melody around it, so that the ground softened and steamed,

'Play on,' said Will. He tapped on the ground with one drum stick, tucking the other stick into his belt, and pressed his fingers into the mud to listen to the earth. Will's fingers felt the pulse of the ground, slow and dark and deep. Wet and steady. The Earth was old and patient. The thing waking in it, though much older than London, was still younger than the ground on which London stood, and younger than the river under which it lay.

With the one hand, Will slowed the rhythm of the tune they were making and sang sweetly to the thing under the mud.

> *Hush thy heart, great beast*
> *Let sorrow fly away.*
> *Dwell thee not on life's great hurts*
> *But rest thee while thee may*
> *Softly still thy mind*
> *Let slumber soothe thy pain*
> *Merciful is winter's end*
> *When springtime starts her reign*

Thomas's playing curled around the beat, but his heart was seething. The result was not a lilting cradlesong but something tight and thick; not a letting go but a squeezing of the fist. Will understood too late. Before he could fall silent, or withdraw, he felt it.

Eyes opened deep in mud and *looked right through him*.

TALES OF THE MINSTREL TONGUE

Will fell back, a gasp of fear trapping frosty air in his lungs. He tried to cry a warning to the piper and couldn't, so that Thomas's surprise at the abrupt end to their cradlesong was all for Will landing arse-first on the ice.

And then Thomas's eyes grew wide and his mouth opened in horror but no sound came out. The piper's hair stood on end, and so did Will's in sympathy as the ice crackled and cracked and began to heave, and he knew, he knew, he *oh God* he knew that the thing that he'd felt looking through him was rising up behind him through the mud and ice, and he knew he would never see the moon or sun or stars again, he would never know warmth or bread again, he would never know love again...

The piece of the Thames on which he sat cracked, heaved, tilted, and he slid down it. One hand still clutched the drum stick, his tabor banged against his back where it hung, the stick in his belt jammed into his ribs.

He crashed into Thomas who had instinctively opened his arms to receive him, and they fell in a tangle on the snow and lay there, arms about each other in terror, for comfort, and looked at the being which had risen from the frozen river.

It almost looked like a man: tall, broad-shouldered, with arms and legs. But its body was made of mud and chunks of ice, pieces of bone and wood. Its chest was the mouldering portion of the prow of an ancient boat, sunk a thousand years ago. Its hair bristled in shards of weed and pottery: clay-brown, glazed blue, fragments of figures and colours.

It shook its bewildered head, scattering sleet. It raised its chin and opened its mouth and howled at the snow-and-ash laden sky.

Hailstones fell. Will and Thomas flung their arms over their heads and they huddled over each other. Fist-sized chunks of ice glanced off their arms, their bodies, bruising them. One struck Thomas on the forehead, drawing blood. Another crashed into Will's fingers and he felt a bone break.

The man of mud with ice blue eyes roared words they didn't understand into the air. Waves of grief and rage rolled off the sound and from its body and through their flesh and somehow within the waves of sound, Thomas heard meaning.

I am cursed. I am wronged. I am doomed.

Thomas struggled to his feet with his blood frozen in a streak down his face, and he roared back at the creature who hadn't even seen them.

'We are all cursed, all wronged, all doomed! We don't all destroy the world!'

The creature ceased howling and tilted its head down then moved it slowly left and right, listening. Its ice blue eyes were unseeing, but its face was wrapped with confusion and irritation.

'What are you to speak to me?' it emanated.

'I'm a man you've wronged.'

'I do not know you.'

'Yet you did me harm. You killed my brother.'

'No,' said the giant. 'Not brother. *Sister*.'

'He was my brother and we killed him, you and I.'

The giant was confused again. 'My brother is dead. I slew him by mistake.'

'I killed mine with negligence, selfishness and fear,' said Thomas. He wept and the tears froze on his cheeks.

TALES OF THE MINSTREL TONGUE

'Loki tricked me,' said the mud-man. 'He gave me a dart of mistletoe, which of all things had never promised not to harm Baldr. All the other gods threw weapons and beautiful Baldr only laughed. I was jealous, I admit. He was so beloved of our mother. One little dart of mistletoe from my hand and he laughs no more. My brother Baldr is slain at my hand.' It howled into the air again then slumped, blind eyes turned towards the musicians. 'Vali killed me in just wrath, but a god never truly dies.'

Will stirred from his watching. He heard Thomas speak to the mud-man, and heard its replies in his blood and bones, through the earth. 'A god, are you? How is it you're here?'

'Loki bound my spirit to an earthen jar. He delivered me to the hands of men to be a talisman. I have travelled far from Asgard on warships, but I never brought those Captains to victory. Another of my brother's tricks. He never tires of them.'

'Baldr?'

'Loki is also my brother.' It frowned. 'He is not always my brother. Perhaps my sister too, sometimes. He takes many shapes.'

'My brother had other shapes before we killed him.'

'I did not harm your brother.'

'A fire on the other side of the world covered the sun with ash and brought a winter cold enough to wake you,' snarled Thomas. 'Now you're killing the world with ice.'

'I am the god of ice,' it said, as though such deaths couldn't be helped.

'Do you have a name, Loki's brother?' asked Will casually.

'I am Hoor.'

'I think I've heard of you,' said Will. 'By the name of Hod.'

'I have many names.'

Thomas scowled. 'Well, Hoor of Many Names, you killed Dickon with your cruel winter.'

'Not alone,' said the ice god Hoor and his tone wasn't kind. 'Negligence, selfishness and fear, you said.'

'That's right,' said Thomas, just as ruthless, 'We're a pair alike, we two. Just as you killed Baldr with envy, foolishness and spite.'

Will held his breath, sure from the fury on Hoor's face that their luck was done and death was coming.

Instead, Hoor laughed, grimly, without mirth. 'I did.'

'I know what you did to Baldr. Shall I tell you my tale?' asked Thomas.

'Did you kill a god?'

'A god can't die, you said, but my sister-brother died twice, first as maiden then as man.'

Hoor bent his head to hear more closely. Will, likewise, listened. His broken finger throbbed but he gripped his drumstick tight anyway, unsure of what to do, or if anything was possible.

'Lulie was born a rosy lass who could never be a maiden. She never learned the skill of it or to desire that she should,' Thomas said. His voice rose and fell in storytelling cadences, but it was filled with the sharpness of a secret's first telling.

'From youth, my older sister would answer to nothing but Dickon. She was boyish in all things, from her large hands and loud laugh to the careless way she ran and climbed and fought with boys who challenged her wildness. Dickon caused our parents only grief, except for when she sang, for then she sounded like an angel.

TALES OF THE MINSTREL TONGUE

'Dickon would not relent in being Dickon, and would not be made to wive, since her body and her heart to womanly virtues would not strive. Dickon grew tall but lean; her menses would not come. At last our parents gave up persuading Dickon to be Lulie and accepted their daughter was a son. As a family, we buried Lulie as a name. Dickon my brother from that day became.'

Will pressed his hands to the earth and ignored the ache of one broken finger while all the rest tapped faintly in the dirt, picking out the uneven rhythm of Thomas's story.

'To me Dickon confessed he'd found a way, a trick of song to make his body obey. To banish his irregular courses and sing his chest flat. I confessed I had my own tricks after that. With my self-made bone and yew pipe I charmed the partridge and the lark to my knife. I fluted fishes to my net, fires to light, clouds to part, warmth to night. We found when I played and Dickon sang, we charmed coins to our purse and our good fortune rang.'

Will felt the dirt under his fingers tremble, though Hoor was, like him, transfixed by the story. Will found in it echoes of a ballad heard last summer. The long tale written by a sarcastic Cornish poet going by Heldris. In the tale, an earl's daughter was raised as a boy named Silence. 'The boy who is a girl' – *li vallés qui est mescine* in the poet's hand. What else had the ballad contained? *Jo cuidai Merlin engignier, Si m'ai engignié.* 'I thought to deceive Merlin but I have deceived myself'.

Will already knew this similar story of Dickon didn't end well. Yet the story compelled, as did Thomas's telling of it.

'We brothers thought it easier to sing for wealth than learn our father's trade, and we did well, until a burning mountain this early winter made. Will says the cold stirred you from your sleep. You brought a bitter cold and we starved, and so my brother's magic grew weak.'

All Thomas's rage seemed now self-directed, the nails of his own curled fists biting into his palm, drawing blood. The vibration in the earth under Will's hands shuddered.

'Dickon dared not carouse with pages and with squires, the body he'd shaped for himself did not hold true. But I was cold and wished for the warmth of other companionship, and the cheerful comradery that ale and wine imbue. I wished to forget, with men like me, that men may die of want. To spend a night without Dickon's fear and rage for his body changing, thin and gaunt. So I went to the woods with other men and wasted life and time, and burned fuel that should have had more prudent use, and fed on Hanley's stolen bread and wine.'

Thomas's chest was heaving as though he had climbed mountains to tell his tale. His body was trembling with the strength of his feeling, which fortunately also masked the insistent tapping of Will's nine healthy fingers on the ground. Will was getting the hang of the rhythm now, thrumming under the surface of the earth, under the surface of Thomas's tale, and under the surface of the ice. A small magic, unheeded as yet by the blind monster.

TALES OF THE MINSTREL TONGUE

Will thought he saw something moving in the air, a flap of dark wings. He thought he felt something moving in the sluggish water under the ice, a deep river green. He didn't let himself be distracted, but continued to tap the beat and listen to the words Thomas spoke. There was no spell in them yet, but for all that, they were spellbinding. Hoor, unspeaking, listened hard to every word.

'I returned, drunk, to find Lord Hanley, seeking his unfaithful staff, discovered my poor Dickon whose face and body were womanly round and soft. He could not find the thieves of wine and wood, so he punished the one who had lied to him, though done less harm than good. He locked Dickon in the snow and ice in a pen beside the woodshed, and that's where I found my brother-sister frozen, where he fell and broke his dear head.'

The air almost hummed with the tension of this ending, the death of Dickon.

'Negligence, selfishness and fear,' said Hoor. 'But yours was not the hand that slew your dear.'

Did Hoor know he'd spoken in this land's English tongue, and made a rhyme to add to the magic all around?

'Yet I'm culpable. Dickon died because of me. He also froze to death because of you. The fault is ours to share or refuse equally. You who your brother with envy, foolishness and spite slew.'

Hoor's voice rumbled in its chest of mud and ice and bone, a dark agreement at the remorse.

'What should we do, we guilty brothers?' Thomas asked. 'Would our own deaths make amends for what we've done?'

'I will find redemption or annihilation at prophesied Ragnarok. What fate do I deserve? What should my fate become?'

'Await your final reckoning undisturbed in the mud.'

Will's hands had taken up the rhythm from his aching fingers. His broken finger was swollen but numb. He had begun to hum under his breath.

Hush thy heart, great Hoor

'I am weary with the waiting,' grumbled Hoor. His ramshackle face began to sag.

'Become undone, as was my brother in his blood,' said Thomas, only he was singing now. Will sang softly beneath Thomas's loud, clear voice.

Hush thy heart, great Hoor
This body be not thine

'What are you doing?' demanded Hoor.

Dwell thee not on rage and pain
This England is not thine.

Wet earth and mouldering rubble sloughed away from the body Hoor had made for himself. For a brief moment, he diminished – then, alarmed, enraged, he opened his muddy maw and roared. His body began to form again. Made of mud, stone, ice, bones and the waterlogged hulls of sunken ships, he reared up three, four, five times as large as before. God-like truly in his fury, yet like a mortal in his desperation.

He raised his arms, as if to bring them smashing down.

TALES OF THE MINSTREL TONGUE

Thomas's voice joined with Will's then. Neither had sung this song before, yet the words came to them both, the magic of earth and air combining, and some of water too, where elements of air and earth were entwined in it.

Hoor's arms remained up, his feet melded with the riverbed, straining to move. Unmoving. Arrested by the magic in the music.

A flash of dark feathers caught the periphery of Will's vision again as he drummed the earth, hard now, feeling nothing but the slam of his palms against the cold ground and the slam of his grieving heart against his chest.

A raven's cawing voice suddenly accompanied them, making words in a creaking undertone.

No god may truly perish
Great Hoor, you cannot drown

Hoor's blind-eyed face lifted to the sky, then dropped. A groan vibrated through the air, Hoor's protest against the song-spell that was undoing his Thames-hewn body.

Surrender to the water
Let slumber take thee down

The mud and bones, the ice and rocks and lumber sagged to a sodden mound. In the centre of the mound was a stone jar sealed in stone, silver and amber. The swell of the jar's body was carved with runes and symbols. A carved archer's bow was etched tightly bound in stylised strands of mistletoe around the centre, spreading up and over the seal.

Wings flapped and a large raven alighted on the ground between Will and Thomas.

'Drum on,' it croaked at Will, then cocked its head at Thomas. 'Your undoing and unwaking song is good. Sing again.'

Thomas sang again. Will beat the rhythm and sang a harmony to make the song stronger.

The raven tapped its beak on the jar, and the amber in it glowed, the silver shone, the stone swelled and thickened, so that the finest crack between seal and jar was rendered seamless.

Then the raven seized the edge of the jar and flapped its wings, tipping the jar over into the turmoil of mud and melting ice. It cawed at the river.

The monstrous shape that Will had earlier sensed roiled strangely under the thinned ice. It heaved, and was gone. Afterwards, Will could not name what he saw. It writhed like a serpent, but was large and thick and scaled, and long ribbons of hair, or weed, had streamed from it. A great, dark maw full of teeth had opened, and shut, and then it was gone. The stone jar, too.

The raven hopped and swept its wings down, rising, then it flew across the frozen Thames, following the shadow of the thing beneath the ice. When it reached London Bridge, the raven came to rest on one of the great curved starlings, filled with rubble packed around the pillars of the bridge for support. It clicked its beak and made sounds which Will could hear from the riverbank. Now a more trilling call, now a sharp caw, and then a strange warbling.

'Did that raven truly speak to us?' Will asked Thomas softly.

'We've sung a god into a pot, and you ask about a talking raven?'

TALES OF THE MINSTREL TONGUE

'It seems the easier discussion,' confessed Will.

Thomas grinned at him, mad-gleeful. 'Then yes, brother Will. I believe the raven who is singing to the river spoke to us.'

Will nodded. 'And the god?'

'Sung to sleep into a jar, as far as I can tell.'

'Good. Good. And we're still alive?'

'Yes.'

'However did we manage these miracles?'

Thomas looked down at the instrument he held in his hand. 'With a yew pipe.'

'I never even got to use my drum.'

They fell silent again as the raven at the bridge took flight, returning to them. As it approached, Will could already feel the air becoming less cold.

The raven alighted on Will's drum where it lay on the ground.

'Hoor was never very clever. You don't have to be Loki to trick him into his prison,' said the raven.

'What are you?' Will dared to ask.

'I am Heimdal, charged by Odin to watch over his foolish son. I think he meant my name as a joke,' said the raven. It tilted its head to stare at them again. 'Loki's mischief makes trouble for us all. I imagine it will make more trouble for you, as well.'

'What kind of trouble?' Thomas asked, but the bird had launched into the air again.

Above them, the clouds parted and the pale sun gleamed through.

Thomas and Will watched the bird fly east towards the Tower of London keep.

'Should we warn King Henry that a magic raven is living in his tower?' Will asked.

'I think we should leave London, as Heimdal the Raven suggests.'

Will fetched his drum, which he slung awkwardly across his back. The action caused his broken finger to throb painfully, feeling having regrettably returned to it. He cradled his hurt hand. 'I know a place in Cornwall,' he said. 'I don't know how quickly Loki may learn of today, but I think we can put some miles between us.'

'The raven could be lying.'

'It could be trying to help. It helped us once already.'

'You have a point, Will. Come on, then. Cornwall it is.'

'Or Ireland,' said Will, 'Which is across the sea and therefore further away.'

'Dickon always wanted to see Ireland,' said Thomas.

'Then let's see Ireland, for Dickon.'

Thomas and Will fell into step, side by side. By the time London had finally stirred to the thawing day, the minstrels had left the city walls far behind.

THE RAVEN PERCHED ON the tip of the London Bridge starling, watching the elephant crossing the frozen Thames down by Blackfriar's Bridge.

TALES OF THE MINSTREL TONGUE

'I thank you for coming,' he said to the man and woman behind him. They were all three watching the fair taking place on the ice. Sheep were roasting with a sign declaring them 'Lapland mutton'. Two men were charging sightseers to watch the spectacle, plus a shilling for a slice. Elsewhere on the ice, gambling huts and tents for drinking houses were making the most of the novelty. A printing press was turning out terrible poetry on thick paper, boys were playing skittles, and a swing named The Sky Lark was filled with giggling courting couples. The spectacle was new to the eyes of the man and woman with the raven, though they'd read of such things.

The raven had seen it all before.

'You humans can't resist dancing on ice,' it said, ending the pronouncement with a caw made of equal parts admiration and impatience. 'Your Kings and Queens especially. That fat Henry the Eighth, and then his red-headed daughter. And now here is your paunchy Prince Regent, poking at the ice with no care for what's beneath it. Anyone would think Erra Pater's prophecy had never been printed, eh Lily?'

'We were never sure that was a prophecy,' said Lily Thorn, drawing her thick winter coat more closely about her. In her left hand she gripped a bundle wrapped in soft leather. Erra Pater's ridiculous lines of poetry, scribed in 1684, were often analysed in her family's journals, but no conclusion had ever been reached.

Lily's companion, equally snugged against the cold, crouched on the broad base of the starling, which created a bulwark for the pylon and foundation of bridge. A fiddle and bow were tucked under his arm. 'The lines 'and now the struggling sprite is once more come, to visit mortals and foretell their doom' suggests knowledge of the HoorFrost.'

'Not all songs are magic, Guy, and not all doggerel claiming to foresee is a prophecy,' countered Lily.

'Yet here we are again,' said Guy Hawk drily, 'Trying to keep an ice god asleep in a jar.'

The raven gave the ice below the starling his full attention.

'She doesn't mean to regurgitate the thing,' it said, 'It's not easy to swallow a god and keep it down. And these two bridges' – it meant London Bridge and Blackfriars, where the elephant was stepping back onto the banks – 'slow the river's flow too much in winter, so it freezes, and frost is Hoor's element. Makes the runes burn on the vessel. It's a combination for indigestion.'

There, beneath several feet of ice, was the suggestion of movement. Scales and a sinuous body. Trailing green weeds. Lily wasn't sure how she could see such a thing, or even if she had. Yet the knowledge was certain. She had inherited more than Thomas Rowan's minstrel voice and his pipe through the preceding generations.

Guy rose to his feet and brought up the fiddle. Not long ago, he and Lily had been playing out there among the Londoners on the Thames, but only in part for the coin. Coin was good for bread, but applause was good for magic.

His bow across the strings asked a question of the creature below. The creature moved, rolled. Granted grudging permission.

TALES OF THE MINSTREL TONGUE

Lily had unrolled the package and lifted the pipe to her lips. It was made of yew, a wood said to aid witches to speak with other realms. She'd found it useful in quieting ghosts and banishing demons. Guy's fiddle, birds and vines carved into its body, wasn't made of anything magical, but magic had been played through it for two hundred years. Magic had been sung into it when Gideon Hawk had made it after the 1608 frost fair, replacing the one broken by that year's binding.

Gods were indeed hard to keep bound.

Lily, Guy and the raven all saw then how the creature of the mere rolled under the ice, among its coils a glowing thing. Amber light and silver, and runes pulsing. Hoor was waking up.

Lily played the pipe. The raven called a rhythm with its 'tok tok tok'. Guy's fiddle sang around Lily's fluting notes, the raven's croaking ones, and he sang.

Hush thy heart, Great Hoor
Tis not yet time to wake
The fate of Asgard waits for you
Sleep on, for London's sake.

For over 500 years, the inheritors of Thomas Rowan and William Hawk had come to do this duty. The words changed every time the Thames froze, but the melody persisted, and Hoor was bound afresh. They sealed the cracks in the rune-marked jar that held him. The river's guardian grudgingly opened her maw and re-swallowed Hoor's prison, then sank again down through icy waters to burrow into the mud at the foundation of the bridge.

When the verses were sung and the creature with a god in its belly subsided, Lily and Guy put their instruments away. Walking carefully on the ice, they followed the raven back to the banks.

'We should warn these people off the river,' Guy noted. 'The journals say the ice always melts quickly after Hoor's put back to sleep.'

'We should get this bridge knocked down so it doesn't slow the water to ice and keep waking the old bastard,' croaked the raven.

'Can we do that?' Lily asked.

The raven's feathers ruffled in a shrug. 'I heard talk of rebuilding the bridge, last time they were clearing ravens from the Tower.'

'Heard talk or suggested it?'

The raven let loose a sly cackle. 'Perhaps it's as you say. Perhaps I'm suggesting other things too. It's annoying and inconvenient when they clear the ravens out. The Tower is my best view of Hoor's prison, after all. It's not a lie to say England may fall if the ravens are made to leave.'

Lily stamped her feet on the banks to shake the snow off her boots. She didn't look at the raven when she spoke. 'Are you the same raven all our ancestors write about? Are you Heimdal?'

The raven laughed again. 'What makes you think I would be?'

She bravely raised her head to look at it. 'Nothing makes me think you aren't.'

The raven only laughed again and took flight, returning east to the Tower.

Guy stamped his feet too, seeking warmth. 'If it's Heimdal, he's over 550 years old.'

'If it's not Heimdal, it knows a lot about all the other times our family has been called to bind Hoor again.'

'Perhaps ravens have journals, like we do.'

Lily finished wrapping the pipe in the soft leather again then adjusted her bonnet. 'Don't be foolish, Guy.'

Guy only grinned at her. 'It's in my nature to be a jester, Lily Thorn.' He offered her his elbow, though. 'Let's go call to these ice-mad revellers to beware of the thaw, and then find a place for supper, shall we?'

Lily, having pulled her gloves on, slipped a hand into the crook of his elbow. 'Oh God, yes, tea. And then I'll record today's binding in the journal.'

'You're a conscientious minstrel,' said Guy, dropping a light kiss on her gloved hand.

'One of us has to be,' she teased, but her mouth had dimpled in a smile.

AUTHOR'S NOTE: The poem about 'Silence' that Will reflects on is *Le Roman de Silence*, written in the first half of the 13th century but not rediscovered until the 20th.

Stitch and Witch

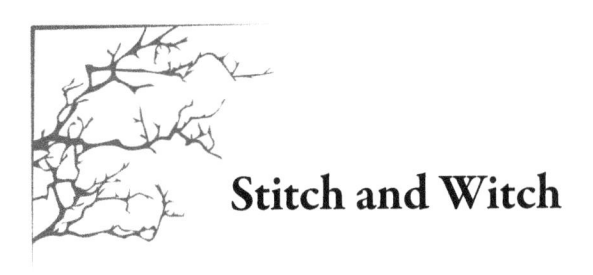

Jay Scheller didn't have long to regret his decision to summon a demon. For one brief minute, as he drew a sigil with his bleeding palm over the chalk pentagram, he wondered if this was really the wisest way to get 'rich, laid and lucky'. But then his open wound dripped across one pale line, breaking the cursed confinement, and in an instant he got his wishes.

The many-limbed demon thrust sixteen priceless gold-tipped talons into Jay's belly, laid him out on the concrete garage floor, and Jay was very lucky to be dead before the demon ate his heart.

For dessert, the demon devoured the printout that the late and delicious Jay had downloaded from the internet. Then it flapped its bone wings and, tentacles waving, it escaped into the night to look for crunchy, screaming snacks in Appleby-on-the-Wold.

NARRELLE M. HARRIS

A DEMON CAN'T SET CLAW in a British shopping centre without exciting comment. When it starts biting the heads off punters too slow to flee, certain groups of people hear about it very quickly indeed. Those with the Minstrel Tongue, for instance – people bearing nature's gift of magic in song, to help keep the balance of light and dark in the world.

Of course, the number of Minstrels is tiny, per square acre, and even with a magic larynx and a seasoned instrument, it takes time to reach the trouble spots. Fortunately for the inhabitants of Appleby-on-the-Wold, Agnes Penney's knitting circle knew what to do.

Elena Clemons had been selecting some beautiful Irish Zwartbles yarn (both absolutely vital to her knitter's soul and absolutely surplus to her stash) when a severed – or rather, chewed – limb hurtled past the shop window. She fled, calling Agnes as she did.

'Another idiot's summoned a demon. We've really go to get that website shut down.'

'I'll call the other others. Any idea which demon?'

Elena held up her phone in selfie mode and took a picture of whatever was behind her. The camera couldn't cope with the image any more than the human mind could, but the hint of tentacles, golden claws and wings of bone were enough.'

Azhathak.

Neither said his name out loud. That was literally asking for trouble, until they were prepared.

'I have to get my book,' said Elena.

'I'll get the room ready,' replied Agnes, with a bitter sigh.

TALES OF THE MINSTREL TONGUE

THE SIX KNITTERS GATHERED in Agnes' living room. She had the chalk and the candles; Brian Rudge brought the sage and thyme; Elena had the incantation from her ancestral grimoire; 18 year old Dylan Thorpe, new to the crew, brought some wool he'd spun and dyed himself at the family farm; and Treat Hawkins brought their beautiful voice and crow feathers. Dot Melling, hands too knotted now with rheumatoid arthritis to knit, had brought the scones.

Brian arranged five chairs at the points of the pentagram Agnes had drawn on her polished wooden floor.

'There go the floorboards again,' she sighed, dwelling on the nub of her bitterness.

'We could put down a tarp,' suggested Treat.

'I tried that once. One of the candles got knocked over, the tarp caught alight and it set fire to the wallpaper. It's fine. I'll throw a rug over the parquetry when we're done.'

Brian smoked the space over the pentagram and all around the chairs with a sage smudging stick. He even smoked the knitting circle in general. Dylan sneezed.

'Dude, watch it! Allergies, man!'

'Sorry, sorry.' Brian, a big, gentle man, patted his skinnier compatriot's shoulder and moved on. 'Dot, you want me to smoke the scones?'

'Leave them be, Brian. I blessed the flour and the butter before I started.'

'Any news what that blasted beast is up to now?' asked Agnes, putting the chalk away and setting the candles at the each point of the pentagram. That done, and the wicks lit, she checked the baskets of yarn beside each chair. She was pleased that Dylan had brought his wool: being handmade by the knitter, the result of their work would definitely be stronger.

Elena had been building up the requisite spells in her head, moving her lips but making no sound as she stored them at the back of her mouth. At the word 'beast', her tongue burned, but she was too experienced to let it spill. She waved at Treat, who held up the shopping centre livestream on her phone.

'It's gone to the gym at the east end of the shopping centre,' Treat said. 'The police have no idea what to do with it.'

Dylan was puzzled. 'I thought it fed off laziness?'

Agnes tutted. 'Laziness is an attitude, not an activity. It's probably looking for the ones who drove there.'

'Judgemental, much?'

'It's a demon. That's its job.'

'Time to do ours,' said Elena, and they all took their seats.

The summoning began with the clackety-clack of five pairs of needles: casting on, leaving a long, long tail of yarn; one long row (faint *clackety-clackety*), the next (*clackety-clackety*), onto the right needle (*clackety-clackety*), then onto the left (*clackety-clackety*), then right again, then left (*clackety-clackety, clackety-clackety*).

The five of them worked fast, keeping pace, row for row. Soon they had each knitted twenty rows, then forty. Dot moved anticlockwise around the circle, taking up the long tail of yarn, threading it through a darning needle and sewing it firmly into the next person's piece.

Each knitter's piece was a different colour; each had the tension given it by the individual maker. Each was crafted with the maker's gifts. The sage and thyme that Brian had grown in his own garden was wrapped around his moss green yarn. Dylan's buttercup yellow, hand-spun yarn held the essence of his strong, kind and clever hands. Ellen muttered words of the old incantation, breathing their power into her night blue wool. Agnes used her oldest needles, the ones passed down from mother to daughter for generations, on her pastel pink yarn. Treat wove the crow feathers, volunteered by the talkative flock who watched over their yard, into rows of royal purple as they knitted.

Treat also sang: not words but harmonies. Their voice ravelled up the click of the speeding needles and the rustle of the balls of yarn turning in their baskets; the faint crackle of burning candlewicks and the sizzle of the wax; the quiet crunch of herbs bound up in fibre; Dot's footfall as she walked widdershins around the circle, checking that no thread was pulled loose; Elena's muttered words spooling out of her mouth like spun thread.

Humans are nimble; the fastest of them can knit at a stitch a second.

Agnes and her knitting circle were faster than that, urged on by Treat's song, Elena's spell, Agnes' heirloom needles. Now that each piece was linked, those three things worked with every other thing and the rows cascaded from their flying hands.

Agnes's great-great-great-grandmother was the one who learned that the magic of the Minstrel Tongue was not restricted to musical instruments and melodic voices. She learned it when a vampire cut her throat with a dirty thumbnail. She lived, but her voice was murdered. Not a peep could she make with her throat, but she'd always been the troupe's drummer, and she found the percussion of the needles as she knitted through her convalescence was enough.

Let the Minstrels have the roads and byways, great-great-great-grandmother Prudence had decided. The Yarners would watch over the hearth.

Elena reached the end of her chant and closed her lips on any further sound, holding the roiling echoes of words behind her teeth. Simultaneously, each of the other knitters ceased their *clackety-clackety*.

In the centre of the pentagram, without lightning or smoke or stench, stood the demon Azhathak, its gold-tipped talons and open maw bloody, its countless eyes staring.

Agnes tilted her glasses down to the end of her nose so she couldn't see it so well. The others had closed their eyes.

'*You summon me?*' Azhathak hissed.

'Go home, foul fiend, is, I think, my line,' said Agnes.

Azhathak's many thousand teeth glinted. '*Make me.*'

'Unmake you, more like,' muttered Dot crankily.

Azhathak sneered at her, flicked its long tongue in her direction, tasting her life and her pain. Dot put her fingers to her ear and fiddled behind the lobe.

'*Dorothy Mary Smith, you old bag of bones. Husband and sons all dead and gone. They'd rather be rotting meat than spend another day with you.*'

TALES OF THE MINSTREL TONGUE

Dot smiled tartly at the demon and tapped her ear. 'Hearing aid is off, you nasty little bugger.'

Agnes nodded and the circle began to knit again.

Azhathak's disdain rolled off it like a miasma. '*You've brought fleece to a soul fight.*'

The circle kept knitting, faster than ever. *Clackety-clackety*.

Elena opened her mouth for the spell to spill out again, the charged words falling with her breath over her wool. Treat hummed the sounds of the room into harmony – even Azhathak's whines and snarls as it realised that it could not tempt one of the seated knitters to break the lines of the pentagram.

The *Clackety-clackety* of the needles blurred into a percussive ticking, a million grasshoppers, a million click beetles, a million bird-beaks snapping at once.

A thread of silver light wove from Treat's lips into the wool on her needles; spread from there to every knitted length on every pair of moving needles in the circle. The silver thread of light wound itself through the patterns in each piece which, if Azhathak had thought to look, were not simple stitches but made of patterns and knots.

Elena's spell was inside the stitching, a code, a message, a cage, a binding.

Azhathak tried to bargain with them. It wheedled and offered great treasures, but the circle drowned it out with the blurred clamour of *clackety-clackety-clackety-clackety-clackety-clackety-clackety-clack*.

Then the circle rose as one, the woollen lengths they'd knitted trailing on the floor. While they knitted furiously, Dot walked widdershins, ensuring as one ball of wool neared its end another was tied to it, and so they kept knitting.

And then the trailing ends rose on the crackle of the silver magic woven into the stitches, lifting between the five and raising a spell-soaked net up above Azhathak's head.

Azhathak snatched at it with golden claws, determined to shred it to threads and ribbons. Instead, it activated the binding. Night blue and buttercup yellow and moss green and baby pink and royal purple tangled around its claws and feet; bound up its arms and tentacles and teeth. Wrapped across its many many many eyes.

The circle knitted, Elena chanted, Treat hummed, and Azhathak twisted and turned, hissing like fat in a fire. The yarn doubled and trebled and increased a hundred fold and wrapped Azhathak in a colourful cocoon that held tight as steel and soft as clouds and the demon's struggles only made the binding tighter.

At last, like a fly spun in a spider's web, cocooned Azhathak lay curled in the middle of the pentagram.

The knitters cast the yarn off their glowing needles.

The sound of knitting – *clackety-clack* – continued all around them, tangled with a whisper of the spell and the hum of the room's harmony.

Moving as one, like it had been rehearsed, the five raised their knitting needles high and then plunged them down into the twitching bundle, without a toe crossing a single chalk line.

A gelatinous pop, the smell of burned wool, and the cocoon of blackened yarn sank, empty, to the ground.

TALES OF THE MINSTREL TONGUE

The only sound was the crackle and hiss of the candle flame, reminiscent of drizzling, pinprick rain pattering onto on canvas.

Dylan, shaking, said, 'That was intense.' He shook the needles in his hands, shaking off the remnants of demonic banishment. 'These were my favourite needles.'

'They'll be stronger now,' Agnes assured him. Her own heirloom pair was a shade darker, as they'd darkened every time they sent a demon back to the depths.

'No dropped stitches?' Elena asked.

Dylan was the only one who twitched. 'No, but it was close,' he confessed. 'I've never knitted that fast before.'

'Almost isn't the same as actually dropped,' Brian said, always the encourager. 'Good job, lad.'

'A dropped stitch only leaves a loophole for a demon to return sooner,' Agnes explained, though this was a very simplified version of the consequences of a dropped stitch. Dylan was doing well; no need to petrify him to trauma with all the little details right now, especially as he hadn't made a mistake.

Light flooded the room – Dot throwing the curtains back and pushing the windows open to let air in and the unmade demon fug out.

'I'll put the kettle on, will I?' she said, 'Brian, dear, will you set out the plates. And you,' she slapped Dylan's wrist as he went to sneak a scone. 'Wash your hands, or it'll all taste of sulphur.'

Agnes wiped her needles and put them away, well pleased with the day.

Dylan returned, hands scrubbed pink, with a grin. 'The Dread Circle of Yarn strikes another victory for good!'

'For balance,' Elena corrected him. 'Keeping evil down is like a yarn stash. There's always more where that came from.'

The Blue Hour

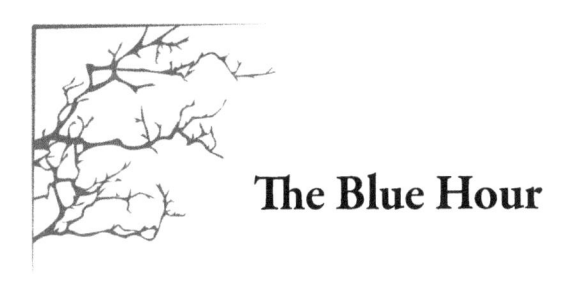

A dusty Holden utility hove to next to the Drawback Creek general store. The tangerine sun was a molten ball of light, about to ooze along the horizon as it set. Soon it would be golden hour, beloved of photographers – the intense yellow light would flare and spill into grades of orange across clouds and land, lending the air a magical golden glow. Even Drawback Creek could look beautiful when that light burnished the tiled roofs and the tops of the eucalypts and the metal shields over the streetlights.

'Here ya go,' shouted the driver to his passengers in the tray of the ute. 'Sure you wanna get off here?'

'I'm sure,' said the pale, young, dark-haired woman getting out of the tray. Her dog, an affable white and tan mongrel, leapt down after her and waited while she put on her backpack; picked up her guitar case.

'It's gettin' dark, and Drawback hasn't got a motel or anything. You can stay at my place, about an hour down the highway, if you want. I can bring you back in the morning. When it's daytime. I live with me mum, so no funny stuff, promise.'

'Thanks, but I'm good. I'm from around here,' she said.

'Ah well. Your funeral, I guess.'

'I don't think it'll come to that,' she smiled but her tone contained some doubt. 'Thanks for the lift.'

'No worries,' the driver assured her, and pulled back out onto the long, empty road.

The woman resettled her backpack, adjusted her grip on the guitar case, and looked down at her dog. 'Do you think he's heard about it, Gibson?' she asked. Gibson panted and thumped her tail in the dirt. The woman scruffed the dog's head. 'Good girl. Come on.'

The woman walked passed the general store, closed much earlier than it should have been. A sign, painstakingly hand-drawn, was taped inside the window, the edges of it curling with many months of exposure to sunlight.

Closing 5pm till further notice.
Call Laurie Morrow
for urgent deliveries.
STRICTLY NO DELIVERIES AFTER 9PM.

Beyond the general store was the butcher, a burger joint/fish and chipper, pharmacy, café, the hardware store, a few other small concerns, all closed up tight. Beyond them was the Country Fire Authority building, ready for the next fire or flood emergency. Opposite that was the Frogmouth Pub. The lights were still on there and muted music snuck through the closed doors.

The reaction when she opened the door wasn't quite like an old-fashioned Western, with the music stopping and the piano player, the drunks, harlots, sheriffs and all frozen to the spot to glare at the newcomer. The jukebox kept playing for a start; and silence only lasted a moment.

TALES OF THE MINSTREL TONGUE

'Kell Wrigley!' shouted an old feller in greeting. 'Jeezus, girl, bin a donkey's age since we saw ya! Come in, quick-sticks, and get that door shut, before the Drawback Devil gets ya!' He laughed raucously, but he was the only one.

Kell ducked inside, called Gibson in after her, and left her guitar by the closed door. 'Hiya, Kev. Still here, eh?'

'Going strong,' he grinned, while the locals and the staff hugged a hello to the town's prodigal daughter.

But then Kev's grin fell away. 'So far, anyway. It hasn't been the same since you left, Kell.'

The silence was momentary, but awkward.

'I couldn't stay,' Kell said at last.

'Nah. Nah, I know.'

'What brings you back, then?' asked Zoe the barmaid. 'I mean, we thought you cleared out for good, after Liam died.'

'Laurie Morrow called me,' said Kell. 'About... about what Katie saw.'

The little crowd fell silent, while the jukebox played Troy Cassar-Daly singing 'Things I Carry Around'.

'He said she's not the only one who...who's seen him.'

'Bloody nonsense,' said Kev.

'Just ghost stories,' said Mick Meacham. 'Nobody believes in 'em.'

'I saw him,' said Zoe abruptly. She cast an apologetic yet stubborn look at Kell. 'Liam Morrow, clear as day, when I was walking home one night last month. In his funeral clothes. He tried to talk to me but I ran home and locked the door.' She scowled at her pub regulars. 'I was *not* drunk.'

'Nobody said you were, love,' said Lea Gould, who ran the coffee shop. 'Just tired after your shift. Seeing things.'

'He was *there*.'

'Bullshit,' muttered Kev, and downed his pint.

Kell, mouth dry, swallowed. 'Laurie said Katie saw Liam looking in at the shop from the roadside. Scared her half to death.'

'Been a hard few months on her and Laurie,' said Lea. 'Her heart's not as strong as it was.'

Kell looked at her feet. Gibson whined and pressed against her leg.

'Not your fault, Kell, the car accident; Liam dying like that,' said Mick, returning to his beer.

'I know,' said Kell, 'but...' She left it there. Liam Morrow had meant everything to her. Even after he'd died. Even now. She cleared her throat. 'So... this ghost. Where does he... show up?'

'There's no ghost, Kell,' insisted Mick.

'There bloody is,' said Zoe.

Another silence fell. Some scowled, some sipped beer, some looked at Kell while trying not to seem they were looking.

Kell's hand dropped to scratch at Gibson's head. Zoe put a beer on the counter for her. Kell sipped it, thoughtful. Solemn.

'You got somewhere to stay tonight?' Zoe asked quietly after a while. 'I got a spare bed at my place. There's a room upstairs here, but we haven't let it out in a while. It's a bit musty.'

'Thanks, Zoe. I have somewhere to be tonight.'

Zoe's eyebrows shot up, because it in a small town like this, and haunted as it was, there was nowhere else somebody could be if they weren't staying with a friend. Or sleeping in their car out front of the CFA building.

'I'll be all right. I've got Gibson.'

Everyone looked at the happily panting dog flopped on the floor beside Kell. She didn't look much of a guard dog.

'Well, you know where I am,' said Zoe. 'Come round whenever, if you need it. I'll be in all night.'

'Sure.'

Kell went to pay for her pint, but Zoe waved her away. 'Welcome home,' she said.

Kell's smile was sad, and it seemed clear that she did not intend to stay.

WEARING HER BACKPACK, carrying her guitar case, and with Gibson at her side, Kell walked back through town and beyond, until she reached the gap in the wrought iron fence surrounding the cemetery.

On the left, tall eucalypts grew between the gravestones dating back to the 1870s. The trees among the grave markers on the right were thinner, sparser, with patches of yellowing grass between them. This section contained the burials from the last few decades. Kell made her way to the newest of them, three months old, careful not to step on top of any graves.

Gibson whined as Kell set down her backpack and guitar in front of the headstone which read: *William Morrow, beloved only son. Singing now in heaven's choir.*

The golden hour had almost passed. The light wouldn't fade quite yet. For a short time, with the sun just appearing on the other side of the world, twilight would be washed in blue until it faded at last into darkness.

'It's all right, Liam,' said Kell to the air around her. 'I know you're watching me.'

The shadow she had seen in the far trees moved, but did not emerge.

Gibson sprang to her feet and stared towards the movement. She quivered; gave a muted bark. Whined.

Kell patted the dog then sat on the edge of Liam's grave. She took out her guitar and strummed a few chords.

'It's okay,' she said soothingly, as though speaking to a skittish horse.

A voice croaked back from the shadows: 'It's not.'

Kell gasped, because she wasn't sure she'd expected him to be able to speak. 'No. It isn't. I'm sorry.'

'I don't want you to see me like this.'

It got worse and worse. How articulate he was. How she could read the emotion in his words, just like when he was alive.

'I saw you at the funeral,' she said, determined to be brave. 'We had an open casket. They made you look–' Her voice hitched. 'Almost like *you*.'

'I don't remember.'

'No. You weren't... back yet. Then.' She couldn't bear him hiding from her, however much he may not look like himself. 'Please come out, Li. We have to talk.' She put her guitar aside, on top of his empty grave.

A figure stepped out of the deepening shadows and stood among the Victorian era gravestones. The lingering golden light caught in his blond hair, and it glowed.

TALES OF THE MINSTREL TONGUE

The halo was the only warm thing about him. Liam's skin was terribly, unnaturally, bloodlessly white. It bore unhealed but cuts, held closed with stitches that were concealed under painted tape. Kell couldn't see the wound that had killed him, hidden under his fine funeral suit. The deep slash ran from his right wrist, up his forearm and bicep, almost to his armpit. Sliced open by a torn metal edge of the bonnet, he'd bled out before help could arrive. The fingers of that hand were crooked and didn't move well, limited by the broken bones beneath the skin. His face was grimy; his clothes were wrinkled and smeared in graveyard dirt.

Kell couldn't help flinching, but couldn't help looking at him, either. So altered, yet still her Liam.

'I'm so sorry, baby,' she said, misery in every syllable. 'I didn't mean to raise you from the dead.'

ONE DRUNK DRIVER ON a late, wet afternoon as the sun was setting; one swerve and an overcorrection; one second of calamity; the culmination – three lives lost and a dozen others shattered.

Liam and Kell had been singing and laughing in the front seat of Liam's car, on their way to a gig a few towns away. Gibson and her brother Fender were in the back seats with the guitars, heads thrust out their respective windows, ears and tongues feeling the wind.

Derek Conner had been singing too, a slurring rendition of a Shania Twain breakup song. Tears had blurred the view through the rain-smeared screen and inadequate windscreen wipers. He chugged another swig from his can of Bundy and Coke, and his car drifted sideways. Tyres crunched into the dirt and gravel on the verge, spewing mud everywhere. Derek braked, pulled at the steering wheel back onto the road.

The setting sun flared on the horizon, turning the sheen of water over his windscreen briefly into a golden shield. Derek didn't see Liam's car approaching as his tug on the steering wheel sent him veering into the other lane.

One minute, music, the next, shrieking metal, shattering glass, screams, high-pitched barks, the crunch of one car flung into the trees, the bang!bang!bang! of the other flipping, rolling, coming to rest on its roof.

Derek Conner didn't die of heartbreak, but drowning his heartbreak killed him for sure. It killed Liam Morrow and his dog Fender too.

Kell Wrigley didn't die of heartbreak by the side of the road, once she'd crawled out of the inverted car and realised that her beautiful Liam, her soulmate since they were six years old, was dead, eyes turned unseeing to the stars coming out in the indigo sky.

Gibson limped out of the wreck, curled in her mistress' lap and shivered until the car sent to look for them found the carnage, and called for an ambulance.

TALES OF THE MINSTREL TONGUE

Kell's parents came back to Drawback for the funeral. Kell knew they loved her; that they meant well: but she couldn't bear them being there, interlopers in the house that had been hers and Liam's. She couldn't bear visiting Liam's parents either: they sat in silence together, talking about him, crying, falling into silences filled with unbearable grief.

After the funeral, her parents led her away. She shut herself in her room with Gibson and listened to them plan to take her back with them to Sydney.

Kell climbed out of the window, Gibson at her side, her acoustic guitar on her back. She went to the cemetery and sat by the fresh-turned earth and sang to him.

> *I lost you in the darkness and I want you back*
> *Don't say you can't be with me any more*
> *You stepped into the light that blinded me*
> *And your light was the last thing that I saw*
>
> *How can I follow where you've gone without me?*
> *Where do I find the door?*
> *I know you didn't want to leave without me*
> *Why couldn't you stay anymore?*
>
> *I don't want to be here without you*
> *Come back and we can learn to be more*
> *Don't let that be the last time I saw you*
> *Come back so we can find what our lives were for.*

She poured every grief and every hope into that song. She couldn't have said where the words came from. She just sat and sang her heart and soul to him.

He didn't come back, of course. He couldn't. Liam was dead and buried, six feet underneath her song for him.

The next day, her parents went back to Sydney. Kell went the other direction, with her guitar, her dog, a bus ticket to Melbourne, and a terrible wound in her heart.

She didn't know it, but she took with her a power and left behind its proof.

She found a place to sleep, a place to busk, and some strange people who saw that power in her, and helped to bring it out. Kitty and her bandmates had taught her some surprising things during those three months.

Then she got a call from Laurie Morrow saying that his wife had seen their dead son through the window of the general store.

'YOU... RAISED ME FROM the dead. With a song.'

'I didn't know it at the time. I've found out, since.' Kell could discern the odour of strange chemicals about him. Kitty, who had once worked in a funeral home, had warned her that he might. Told her not to freak out about it. The chemicals had replaced Liam's blood and preserved his organs to delay decay for the funeral. It was all normal. Nothing to fear from the dead, she'd said. Kell wasn't sure what Liam was now, but she wasn't afraid of him.

'How long since?'

'Two days ago. I came back as soon as I could. As soon as I realised.'

'Jeez, Kell. I had to dig my way out.'

Kell went almost as white as he was. 'Oh, god. Oh, Li. I'm-'

'It's been a whole *thing*,' he said, with a sardonic half smile.

'*Don't*, Liam. Don't try to make why I did small. I made a terrible mistake.'

'*I'm* the mistake you made, so I reckon I get to say whatever I want, Kell.'

She swallowed. Nodded. It was only fair. After what she'd done to him. After what he'd endured.

'It's been epically awful,' Liam said, very softly. 'I was so confused. And I knew I wasn't right. I knew I was dead but that I wasn't. I wandered around the cemetery for a few days, after I dug my way out, and I knew I should have been more freaked out, but I didn't have a heartbeat or a pulse, so my body couldn't *feel* anxious, even though my head did. I tried talking to some people, but I was scared to go up to anybody in the daylight. I know what I look like. But at night people thought they were seeing things from drinking too much, or from sadness, or whatever.'

'Oh, Liam.'

'I... sometimes go to look at what people are up to. I miss them. But I can't go back. I tried to see mum and she went into hysterics, and my mum never has hysterics. She's the calm one. Dad had to call an ambulance for her. I can't do that to them again. I stay here in the cemetery mostly. It's not like I need to sleep. To tell the truth, being this – whatever I am – it's mostly really boring. And lonely.'

Kell began to speak, but he spoke over the top of yet another apology.

'Don't tell me you're sorry. Where have you *been*?' Liam's voice was rough; heartbroken. Gibson whined again, a warning underneath her puzzlement.

Kell looked up into the deep brown eyes of the boy she loved. 'I couldn't stay after you died. So I... ran away, I guess.'

'How did that work out for you?'

'Better than I deserved,' she confessed. 'I discovered magic.'

Liam blinked slowly. 'I'd call bullshit,' he said drily, 'except...' He spread his arms to demonstrate the existing strong evidence that magic was real.

Kell took a breath. She'd been rehearsing this part all the way from Melbourne to Drawback.

'I was busking in Melbourne to make the cost of a hostel for the night, when this Japanese woman came up to me. Yuka said I had something special in my music and that I should meet up with her band. They could give me a place for the night too, and they were fine with Gibson there, and she seemed pretty cool. So I went with her and met the others. Kitty's their lead singer. We jammed together a bit and we...' She puffed a laugh of remembered wonder. 'We made it rain in the living room. It was weird. And wet. So then we sang another song together to dry everything out. And they explained that I had what they call the Minstrel Tongue.'

'Sounds like a medieval mental health problem,' said Liam wryly.

TALES OF THE MINSTREL TONGUE

'Might be close to the truth, that. Yuka explained that some people are born with this magical power that they wield through music. People with the gift mostly use it to keep balance between the regular world and the supernatural one, she said. That's what they do. They've been teaching me about it. Helping me to control when it comes out in my music, so that it's directed with intent.'

'So what happened to me?'

'I didn't know my song had real magic in it, until your dad called to tell me about your mum. Even then I didn't fully understand, until I told Yuka and the others about the call. They knew straight away what was going on. They explained that I must have called you back with that song, because I didn't know that that's what I was doing – and it's not something that can ever be done right. Life and death don't work that way, and neither does the magic.'

'I still don't understand what you've done to me, Kell.'

She could hardly face him, but couldn't bear not to. She folded her hands in her lap and tried to be clear.

'Yuka says when you sing with your Minstrel voice, to change the world with magic, you have to put clear intentions into it. Like... with the song that made it rain in the house. If you don't include lyrics about the rain stopping, then it won't, for days and days. Their bass player says he nearly caused a flood once, because he forgot to sing the verse that says the rain stops. When I sang to you, I filled my voice with...wanting you. I didn't think to sing about you being alive like you were before the accident. I just sang that I wanted you to come back to me. I missed you so much. I wanted you back so much. And I put all that wanting into lyrics and music so you'd come back to me. I didn't know it would actually *work*. And what I did was... *this*. I trapped your spirit in your dead body, and I animated you and I told you to come back to me. Not alive, but not truly dead. Just in between. And then I buggered off without waiting for you because I didn't know you'd really come back. And I left you all alone to deal with it.' She looked at her feet, ashamed. 'I understand if you hate me.'

'Couldn't ever hate you, Kelli-Bell,' Liam said softly. Kindly, even. 'Even if you did accidentally make me a zombie. Oh, oh Kell, sorry! Don't cry! I'm joking!'

'I know,' Kell choked on a half-laugh, half-sob. 'Your stupid jokes. I miss them so much. I miss you so much. I wanted you back but I made you a zombie even if Kitty said that's not really what you are but I did, and you're here and I've missed you so much and...'

She subsided, crying into his shoulder as he folded her in his cold arms, held her against his wrecked body, and rubbed her back with hands that bent all wrong.

'My Kelli-Bell, baby, shhh shhh, there, there, it's going to be okay.'

At their feet, Gibson dropped to the ground to look at them both, her tail wagging hopefully.

'I know you'd never mean to hurt me,' Liam said. 'You never meant to frighten me.'

'Never.'

'I love you, Kell. My Special-K.' he pressed a kiss to her forehead. It felt almost like it used to.

They sat together for a little while, Liam with an arm around Kell's back, she resting her head on his shoulder.

TALES OF THE MINSTREL TONGUE

The golden light had faded at last. A melancholy blue light washed over them instead, the last of the sun's light from over the horizon.

'What do we do now?' Liam asked.

Kell was very quiet, and then she said, 'I asked the band what I should do if I'd really sung you back, and they've said... I can't give you your real life back. There's no magic strong enough to sing you back to that. You... your body will decay. Slower than usual, but it will. Steve – he's the oldest and most experienced with the magic – said we have options. But it has to be your choice. This time, at least, I know what I'm doing and you get to choose.'

Liam looked down at Gibson and held a ruined hand out to her. She licked his fingers in greeting and whuffed at him, recognising him even though he was all wrong now. 'You miss Fender do you, girl? Me too. I miss her and you and my Kelli-Bell.' He met Kell's gaze. 'So what are the options?'

'You stay as you are. Here if you want, but you can come with me. Anywhere you like, for as long as we can. It'll get harder, but they taught me some songs to help preserve your body. Steve thinks that might give us a few months, at least. We can go on the road, like we always planned.'

'Not sure I can sing now, Kell. I know for damned sure I can't play the guitar any more, with this.' He held up his misshapen fingers.

'But it's one option. We get more time, at least.'

'The other option?'

'I can help you to let go. To...leave.'

'Die again, you mean. For good.'

She bravely held his gaze, because he deserved her courage in all of this. 'Yes. But you don't have to choose it. You can stay with me.'

Liam laughed ruefully. 'Three months ago I would have, I think. But I've been... 'living' isn't the right word, I guess. But I've had a lot of time to think while I hung around the town. Most nights lately, I sit in the dark, looking up and wishing I was ... up there with the stars. Or I sit in the sun and wish I was like these other bodies, going back to the earth, or like the really old graves with trees growing practically on top of them. I always liked the idea of being part of the world after I died. Earth to earth, like they say. I don't want to be sad and scared any more. I think... I think I want to be part of the cycle again. Not trapped outside of it, terrifying my mum half to death, freaking out my old friends. Riling up the dogs. The dogs who aren't Gibson, anyway.'

Liam looked up at the moon, beginning to glow in the indigo sky, then back at Kell. 'Can you do that for me? Let me go, like that?'

So much of Kell wanted to say no. She couldn't let him go. She wanted him to come with her, to be with her for as long as they could manage it.

But that was all about her and what she wanted, and as Sal had gently pointed out, she and Liam had already had as long as they could get together. The world wasn't always kind. It didn't always let everyone have as much time as they wanted.

But they'd had their time together. Best friends since kindergarten, in love so long she didn't know when they had changed from childhood besties to partners for life.

TALES OF THE MINSTREL TONGUE

'Yes. I can do that for you, Li, baby. Kitty taught me a song for that.'

'Kitty. Sounds like a fluffy name for a girl who sings magic.'

'She's not a fluffy person. She's kind. They're all kind. Yuka, Steve, Aaron, Sal, Laszlo. The Minstrel Tongue's a difficult gift and they're all different kinds of sad, but they're all kind.'

Liam nodded. He sagged a little, and she put her arms around him this time, and hugged him.

'Can you do it now?'

Too soon.

'Yes. If you want.'

'Please. It's so good to see you again, Kell. I'm glad you're here with me. But I think it's time to go.'

'Okay.' She kissed his cheek, then his forehead. 'I love you.'

'I love you too, my Kelli-Bell.'

She picked up her guitar again and settled it across her body.

'Should I...stand somewhere?' he asked. 'Sit on the grave?'

'Sit wherever you'd like to be. Look at something that makes you happy.'

'Oh, that's easy, Kell.' Liam sat opposite her and gazed, smiling, into her face. He became serious. 'Will it hurt?'

'No. It'll be just like going to sleep.'

'Okay. Hey,' he reached out to pat Gibson, who had pressed against his knee. 'It's okay, girl. I'm going now. Maybe I'll find Fender and give her your love. You stay here and look after Kell for me, eh?'

Gibson rested her chin on his knee, and he scratched her some more.

'Good girl.'

Kell had begun to play the song that Kitty had taught her.

'Just listen. Relax.'
'That's a pretty melody.'
'Yeah.'
'It's gentle. I like it.'
'Are you ready, baby?'
'I am.'
Her eyes on Liam's face, Kell began to sing.

Leave your body with a sigh
Those you've loved must say goodbye
This precious frame, beloved skin
Is just the house that you lived in.

Kitty Carrasco had once sung this song in the funeral parlour where she worked, before she had learned anything about who she was, or the Minstrel Tongue. The dead, dressed for their funerals, were sitting up all around her, rising to their feet. Driven by instinct and the magic in her blood, words rose in her throat and she sang to them.

Kitty hadn't been frightened at all. At that time, her only intent was to have them settle again; to be at peace so that they could offer no more grief to the people who'd loved them. The dead had obeyed her, returning to mortuary tables and prepared coffins, ready to for their families to say goodbye to them.

Return to earth, return to sky
Like stars, your atoms learn to fly
Your bones and flesh, no longer you,
Rejoin the world, make something new.

TALES OF THE MINSTREL TONGUE

But the words promised something more, if the intent could be directed.

Kitty and Kell had together written the words Kell would need, to fill the song with intent so that the magic would be precise. They'd even practised the song together, on a dead possum they'd found beside the road. Because Kell knew that if Liam chose this, she couldn't possibly leave his body behind to be found by his family, friends, community. There had already been too much trauma.

> *Your soul can now be flying free*
> *To make its timeless way*
> *Your flesh and bone, your earthly home*
> *Can now return to clay.*

Liam's smile grew soft. His face shone with acceptance. Peace. 'Love you, Kell. You go and be *great*. For us.'

> *Return to earth, return to sky*
> *Like stars, your atoms learn to fly*
> *Your bones and flesh, no longer you,*
> *Rejoin the world, make something new.*

'Goodbye, Kell.'

His body began to fold, no longer animated. Gibson backed away as Liam's body transformed.

> *Your spirit's of the infinite,*
> *Embrace it with a joyful heart*
> *Your body is ephemeral*
> *Returning to where we all start*

His body was there, and then it was... dust. Like smoke from a campfire. Momentarily, as it dissolved into earth, it held Liam's shape, and then it swirled away to nothing.

Kell kept singing. Liam was gone now, so she closed her eyes, and kept singing.

> *Return to earth, return to sky*
> *Like stars, your atoms learn to fly*
> *Your bones and flesh, no longer you,*
> *Rejoin the world, make something new*

When she stopped playing she sat for a while longer. Then she opened her eyes. Liam was gone, and in his place the soil looked rich, newly turned. A green sapling emerged from it. A gum tree.

Kell stroked a tiny leaf with her finger. Gibson trotted over to her.

'He's gone now, Gib. But we got to say goodbye. We got that.'

The blue hour had come and gone while she sang her Liam's body and soul back into the world in the only way possible, now. As the stars came out, she packed her guitar in its case.

'Might take Zoe up on her offer of a bed for the night, eh Gibson? Then back to Melbourne tomorrow. What do you think?'

Gibson whuffed approval and followed Kell out of the graveyard.

The Harp's Voice

A clink against glass startled Tristen from her doze in the large armchair, made nest-like with hand-crafted blankets and pillows. She rubbed her eyes and blinked at the dying fire. The midnight chill was creeping in through the windowpane, under the front door, and would soon be coming down the chimney if she let that fire go out.

The sound that woke her forgotten, Tristen pushed aside the woollen blanket across her knees and reached for one of her forearm crutches. With it, she heaved herself up and balanced on the leg not embraced by the laced leather calliper. The brace ended in a boot, also tightly laced.

Tristen was glad her grandmother slept. Grandma Hazel meant well, but she was annoyingly prone to acting like Tristen couldn't do things for herself. Now, with a few well-practised manoeuvres, Tristen bent to the wood basket, selected some lighter pieces and dropped them over the grate into the fire. She basked in the growing heat before adding a larger piece, then another.

A repeat of the clink against glass drew her eyes towards the old-fashioned array of little square windows set into the north wall of the cottage. With a hop, she turned towards it.

Another clink. Tristen took up her second crutch, went to the window and unlatched it just as another pebble was dropped against the pane.

A raven stood on the window sill. It shook its feathers huffily and cocked its head to give Tristen a beady eye.

'Perdita! You've been ages.' Tristen ushered the bird in with concern. 'Fire's up again. Let me get you some fruit.'

'I'd prefer meat,' said Perdita, a corvid croak to her perfect English. She flew close to the fireplace and spread her wings out to gather in its growing heat before settling to clean her feathers.

'So would I, but fruit is what I have.' Tristen put aside her crutches to cut a ripe persimmon into small pieces for her companion. 'Did you find anything?'

'Apart from the fact that it's c-c-c-cold out there?'

'Very funny.'

'I could tell you better if I had some meat.'

'I'll fry you up some bacon when we're back home tomorrow.'

Perdita hopped on the spot and flapped her wings in a decidedly approving manner. 'Well, the auguries were right. I met a bat who is not a bat.'

'Oh, terrific. I don't suppose we're lucky enough that it's a vampire's familiar?'

'Alas, no. This bat speaks for Hoor.'

'Speaks for or *looks* for?'

'Both?'

'Did Asgard send it?'

'I don't think so. It brings a message but the little fellow seems to act alone.

'You are being unnecessarily cryptic.'

TALES OF THE MINSTREL TONGUE

The raven cocked her head again, and Tristen knew Perdita was laughing at her.

'All right, so you're a talking raven and guardian of Hoor's prison, and you are in fact necessarily cryptic. Perhaps we can skip to the chase?'

The window rattled, loud and hard, with the unmistakable sound of wings beating against the glass.

Perdita flew immediately up to perch on the back of the chair in which Tristen had earlier fallen asleep. 'Bugger. I told it to wait. Bats have no patience.'

Tristen slipped her arms into the crutches again and moved nimbly to the other side of the room, where she'd left her small lyre harp. Her much larger, much older harp was at home in Mile End in London, but Tristen took this sweet little instrument wherever she went, worn across her body in the leather sling she'd made for it. She put it on now as the rattling ceased.

'Where did it go?'

Perdita flew to the closed window and placed her eye to it. 'Gone. Not away, alas, it... oh dear.' The raven twisted her neck to look... upwards. 'Does your grandmother have a fire in her grate upstairs?'

Tristen allowed time for one very expressive swear word and sat down so she had her hands free for the harp.

She swore again when her grandmother came down the stairs, a bat hanging from the front of her nightdress.

'Tristen. This little beast came down my chimney. It's demanding an audience.'

'Grandma...'

'I knew you weren't here for just a visit.'

'Sorry, Grandma. The tea leaves warned that a portent would manifest at the cottage. I wanted to make sure you were all right.'

'You wanted to see what was coming.'

'I can do both.'

'You can't. You smashed your leg to bits and now you have to sit at home and leave the Minstrel work to others.'

Grandma Hazel never could get her head around the fact that disability didn't mean no ability. Tristen had worked hard to maintain dexterity of a different kind and to hone her music magic. It was one reason she'd moved out of her grandmother's house to her own place, years ago.

Her grandma's disdainful gaze fell down on the little bat, still clinging to her nightgown. The bat's gaze was just as baleful in return.

'I'll banish you,' Grandma Hazel told it. Tristen wished it were that easy.

'Why have you come?' Tristen asked the bat. 'Did you come to free Hoor?'

Perdita flew across the room, cawing a warning to the bat, before alighting on the top of the harp.

The bat released the old lady's nightwear and flapped to the carpet by Tristen's feet.

TALES OF THE MINSTREL TONGUE

Once upon a time, Tristen had been an acrobat with a travelling circus. She had walked wires, swung from ribbons and wings, leapt and twirled across floors, danced across narrow beams. She had balanced on unlikely points, just like this raven upon the crown of the harp. When Tristan fought the creatures of darkness, she was so fast, so clever, that the darkness told stories about her. Her Minstrel magic had been expressed through motion and grace, through the closest a human being could come to flying.

And then one day she stepped into a fight she couldn't win. She'd fallen from a height and shattered the magic right out of her bones. So she'd thought. It had felt humiliating, to have to be rescued, when she had once done all the rescuing.

Her grandparents left the circus life to care for her, in this venerable little cottage, with its thatched roof and tiny glass grids for windows, and all its family secrets.

Tristen had thought she'd wither and die of loneliness and sorrow there, but Grandpa Silas made a harp for her and during that long year of healing, she'd learned a lot of things. She'd learned to channel her magic through the strings of her instrument. She'd learned to walk, with her bad leg laced into the leather brace, and two crutches on her forearms.

She'd learned new ways to fight.

Tristen ran her fingers across the harp strings. She began to pluck a melody, then the harmonies. She sang, crooning to the strings and the air and the messenger on the floor, building bridges between them all.

Listen, listen I will tell you
Speak, speak, I will hear you

NARRELLE M. HARRIS

These words of mine
Become thoughts of thine
And thy will speaks to me too.

The bat squeaked. Tristen played and the squeaks became words in the air, following the melody.

I am come from Asgard.
I fear Váli's heart so hard.
He swears revenge still upon
The grieving, unforgiven one
My winter master, Hoor.

Tristen and Perdita knew the story well. Loki had tricked Hoor into killing his brother Baldr. Asgard being what it was, Váli was born at once and grew in a day, his sole purpose to avenge Baldr's death. Deceived and grieving Hoor had almost destroyed the world with a never-ending winter, until steps were taken to trap him on Earth within a clay vessel, a seal set upon its lid, and give him to the great River Thames to conceal. Perdita was the latest in a line of long-lived ravens who made sure that Hoor could not escape until called to Ragnarok.

Tristen and the bat messenger sang bursts to each other, and it became clear that the bat came with a warning of his own.

Unseasonable, the seasons be
The frost and the sun confused be
The shape of winter
The blooms of spring
May, tangled, set the beloved killer free.

TALES OF THE MINSTREL TONGUE

Global warming was even more dangerous than the brave Greta Thunberg kept telling everyone. It clearly threatened to disrupt Hoor's prison.

Tristen wasn't sure what she and Perdita could do about that, except to be more vigilant and try to speak to the ancient one, the true guardian of the prisoner, who lived in the Thames. The last thing anyone needed was for Hoor to escape and for his inconsolable mourning to doom everyone to frostbitten death.

Tristen did her best to sing her thanks for the warning.

'Open the door, Grandma,' she said at last.

Grandma opened the front door and the bat launched itself into the winter night.

'Bloody Asgard,' grumbled the old lady. 'I wish they wouldn't bother you with it. You're done with all that magic now.'

Tristen was the very opposite of 'done with all that magic'. Her Mile End community depended on her. 'Perdita's the sky guardian,' was all she said.

Grandma eyed the bird grimly. 'Is Váli coming to claim Hoor, then?'

'Not yet. But we have to keep Hoor sleeping in the river, for everyone's protection.'

'I don't know how a lame girl and a vain bird are going to achieve that.'

Tristen wasn't sure either, but she had more faith than Grandma. Grandma had lost most of hers when Black Annis had murdered Silas.

'We'll manage,' Tristen said. 'And I'm not the only Minstrel on the planet. There'll be help if I need it, I'm sure.'

Like the rumours that Rome's Burning was changing their name and line-up, now that Alex and Kurt had died. She'd best make sure she had the bass player's number on speed-dial, though.

Just in case.

Acknowledgements

My thanks to all those who support and inspire me, including Tim, the Pixies, Jehni, Anniene, Josh, and everyone on my Patreon: Adelle; D C Sams; Sarah Remy; Julia Hilton; Kim Fasching; Tim Richards; Kimber; Beck; Carey Handfield; sbbeasley; Adam Salisbury; Alice Harris; Lora Timonin; Melinda McCormack; Milane Duncan-Frantz; Sally; Champagne and Socks; Grant Watson; Jack Fennell; Richard Koehler; Sarah Drosendahl; Tansy Rayner Roberts; and Mike Thompson.

Thank you too, dear reader. And if the mood strikes you, a review on Goodreads or Amazon would be wonderfully helpful, however brief!

IF YOU ENJOYED THESE stories, you might like to try *Kitty and Cadaver*: 'a story of grief, love, vampires, music, magic, secrets and the restless dead', available at most online booksellers.

You might also like to support me on my Patreon at
https://www.patreon.com/NarrelleMHarris

You might also like to hear some of the songs from that book which have been professionally produced by Joshua King at Golden Hour studios, and released under the band name Duo Ex Machina. You can find ten songs (from *Kitty*, the Duo Ex Machina novellas and those inspired by Sherlock Holmes and John Watson!) at:

https://www.youtube.com/@DuoExMachinaMusic

About Narrelle M. Harris

Narrelle M Harris writes crime, horror, fantasy, erotica and romance. Her 80+ works include vampire novels, erotic spy adventures, het and queer romance, Sherlock Holmes adventures, and Holmes/Watson romance mysteries *The Adventure of the Colonial Boy* (2016) and *A Dream to Build a Kiss On* (2018). A queer, paranormal Holmesian book focusing on Mrs Hudson as a menopausal werewolf, *The She-Wolf of Baker Street*, was released in 2024.

In 2017, her ghost/crime story "Jane" won the 'Body in the Library' prize at the Scarlet Stiletto Awards. Other works include *Grounded, Scar Tissue and Other Stories* (short-listed for the 2019 Aurealis Awards), and *Kitty and Cadaver*.

Narrelle was also commissioning editor for *The Only One in the World: A Sherlock Holmes Anthology* (2021) and *Clamour and Mischief* (short-listed in the 2022 Aurealis Awards). In 2023, she co-edited *This Fresh Hell* with Katya de Becerra. In 2024, she co-edited *Sherlock is a Girl's Name* with Atlin Merrick.

Many of Narrelle's books are published by Clan Destine Press and Improbable Press, and her work can be found on Amazon and other online retailers.

For more details, visit:
https://narrellemharris.iwriter.com.au/

Other books by Narrelle M. Harris

Kitty and Cadaver

Rome's Burning is a five-piece band with its roots in the 13th century; a line of musicians gifted with the magic-wielding Minstrel Tongue. For hundreds of years, Rome's Burning and its forebears have used music to protect the world from vampires, trolls, zombies, ghosts, banshees, dragons, water demons and other denizens of the dark.

But after one hellish night in the suburbs of Budapest, Rome's Burning defeated a nest of vampires at a terrible cost; their lead singer and the love of his life are dead, Rome's Burning is no more.

The survivors retreat as far as they can - to Melbourne, Australia - to deal with their grief, decide on their future, find a new leader and, as tradition demands, a new name. Before any of that happens, however, these minstrel-warriors have to find out why the dead keep rising everywhere they go.

Everyone has secrets and some of them might explain what's going on.

NARRELLE M. HARRIS

Praise for *Kitty and Cadaver*

'Oh, I love all about this book! I love the world-building, I love the plot, I love the characters, and I love all the music-related stuff. Having this group of misfit chasing monster with MUSIC! Can anything be better than this? And the characters... oh, they are all so well-drawn, so complex and interesting!' ~ Clau, Amazon.

TALES OF THE MINSTREL TONGUE

The Vampires of Melbourne Series

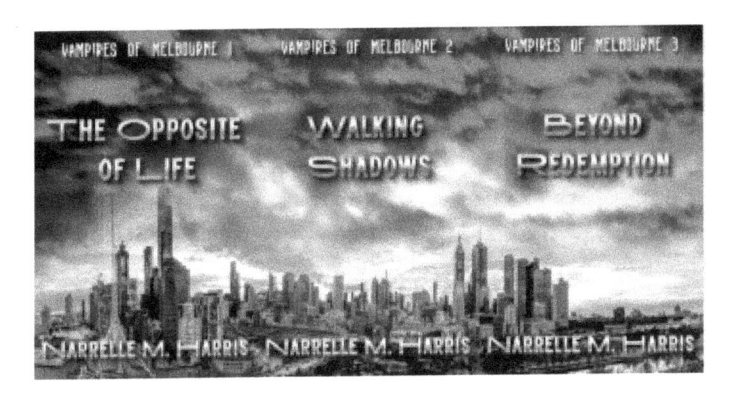

THE OPPOSITE OF LIFE

A very geeky librarian stumbles into a series of murders in Melbourne. In trying to make sense of the deaths and her traumatic past, she discovers that vampires are real – but not all of them are killers. She meets another total geek – the painfully awkward vampire Gary Hooper, whom the vampire community has set onto investigating the deaths. Lissa and Gary join forces to get to the undead heart of the matter and to their surprise find they are becoming friends. But the idea of living forever is a big temptation for someone who has lost so much, and the consequences of this investigation may affect Lissa much more closely than she could have expected.

NARRELLE M. HARRIS

Walking Shadows (*Nominated for Best Long Fiction, Chronos Awards 2012*)

What's an ordinary geekgirl librarian to do when hardcore vampire killers begin killing off Melbourne's vampire population, and her undead bestie is on the hit list? Should she throw herself in mortal danger, despite having no battle skills, let alone supernatural strength? Lissa risks everything to protect someone who should be perfectly capable of protecting himself. And Gary finds that the ways he's changing might make him more human – if they don't get him killed first.

BEYOND REDEMPTION: *coming in 2025*

Lissa Wilson and her vampire best friend Gary Hooper seem to have settled into life and routines after all the drama – but drama is never far away. Gary is increasingly disillusioned with his limitations; Lissa's estranged mother is back in town; and an ex-copper is poking his nose into the whole vampire business. More worryingly, a gangster affiliate of the vampire community is about to disrupt the power balance. Gary and Lissa have another fight of their lives coming up, and everything is going to change.

The Adventure of the Colonial Boy

1893. DR WATSON, STILL in mourning for the death of his great friend Sherlock Holmes, is now triply bereaved, with his wife Mary's death in childbirth.

Then a telegram from Melbourne, Australia intrudes into his grief. 'Come at once if convenient.' Both suspicious and desperate to believe that Holmes may not, after all, be dead, Watson goes as immediately as the sea voyage will allow.

Soon Holmes and Watson are together again, on an adventure through Bohemian Melbourne and rural Victoria, following a series of murders linked by a repulsive red leech and one of Moriarty's lieutenants. But things are not as they were. Too many words lie unsaid between the Great Detective and his biographer. Too much that they feel is a secret.

Solve the crime, forgive a friend, rediscover trust and admit to love. Surely that is not beyond that legendary duo, Sherlock Holmes and Dr John Watson in Narrelle M Harris' *The Adventure of the Colonial Boy*.

NARRELLE M. HARRIS

PRAISE FOR *The Adventure of the Colonial Boy*

'Melancholy, sweet, triumphant, fierce in a beautiful balance.' ~ TA Creech, Amazon

'I found the second reading as exciting as the first.' ~ Heras Mom, Amazon

TALES OF THE MINSTREL TONGUE

A Dream to Build a Kiss On

John Watson, invalided army doctor and sometimes artist, and Sherlock Holmes, consulting detective, become flatmates and friends in contemporary London.

Love grows too, despite past betrayals and present dangers—for where you have Holmes and Watson, there too are Moriarty and Moran.

A Dream to Build a Kiss On, written by Narrelle M. Harris and illustrated by Caroline Jennings, explores love and family, trust and betrayal, brothers and brothers-in-arms, forgiveness and revenge, in an ongoing tale told 221 words at a time.

Praise for *A Dream to Build a Kiss On*

'Exquisite in detail and structure...' ~ Angela Kam White

'A swashbuckling adventure with more twists and turns than a rabbit's warren' ~ Rohase Pierce.

The She-Wolf of Baker Street

AFTER SHERLOCK HOLMES 'rescues' Audrey Hudson from a kidnapper, she offers him her upstairs flat in exchange for solving the unsolved murder of her family in Edinburgh. Sherlock's being forced to theorise without data, however – he doesn't know his new landlady and her late family are werewolves. There's a lot he doesn't know about his attractive new flatmate, John Watson, too.

Momentum is added to the case as Sherlock's investigations suggest a much bigger mystery is at play, involving a disturbing case on Dartmoor with a Greek interpreter; Sherlock's agoraphobic sister, Myca; Audrey's long-dead love, Ruby Stockton; and the fate of Great Britain's mystic heart.

Will Holmes be able to unravel the mysteries that have haunted Audrey's life? And can Audrey protect her new pack, or is she about to lose those she loves once again to unknown enemies?

Praise for *The She-Wolf of Baker Street*

'Brilliantly executed' ~ Ashleigh Meikle

'A touching and unexpected view of 221B Baker Street through werewolf Mrs Hudson's familiar yet brand new eyes' ~ Wendy C Fries

Don't miss out!

Visit the website below and you can sign up to receive emails whenever Narrelle M. Harris publishes a new book. There's no charge and no obligation.

https://books2read.com/r/B-A-RKTUB-MILGF

BOOKS 2 READ

Connecting independent readers to independent writers.